This book belongs to

. . . .

. . . .

CONTENTS

Cover artwork and illustrations for *Rupert and Robo* by Stuart Trotter
Text and couplets for *Rupert and Robo* by Beth Harwood
Designed by Martin Aggett

Endpapers adapted from the *Rupert Annual*, 1967, illustrated by ALFRED BESTALL

THE RUPERT ANNUAL

EXPRESS NEWSPAPERS

EGMONT
We bring stories to life

Published in Great Britain 2011 by Egmont UK Limited
239 Kensington High Street, London W8 6SA
Rupert Bear™: © 2011 Classic Media Distribution Limited/Express Newspapers.
All Rights Reserved.

ISBN 978 1 4052 5708 4
Printed in Italy

Adult supervision is recommended when sharp implements, such as scissors, are in use.

No. 76

RUPERT
and the
Little Plane

Telling how Rupert worked hard so that Willie Whiskers could enjoy his uncle's birthday present.

Illustrated by ALFRED BESTALL
Originally published in the *Daily Express* in 1941

Now Willie's birthday is today,
But, strangely, he's not out to play.

To Rupert's call he pays no heed,
But down the garden runs with speed.

"Whatever scheme is in his head?"
Thinks Rupert, following to a shed.

So, turning home, young Bill he meets,
And him with Willie's story greets;

"I haven't seen Willie Whiskers for ages," thinks Rupert one day. "I do believe today's his birthday. I'll go and see him." Running to the far corner of the village he arrives at Willie's tiny house and reaches for the knocker. Again and again he knocks, but there is no answer. The door of the tiny house opens suddenly and out pops the little mouse. He runs by, holding a large scroll of paper. "Hi, Willie," shouts Rupert.

Rupert is bewildered by Willie's action. "It's not like him to run away from his pals," he murmurs. His curiosity gets too much for him, and he follows the little mouse. By this time there is no one in sight, but noises are coming from a shed. At last he gives it up and wanders away. On the Common he comes across Bill Badger and tells him all the story. "What a queer way for Willie to behave," says Bill.

RUPERT STARTLES WILLIE

Now, armed with wood, the Mouse runs by,
And Bill and Rupert call out, "Hi!"

Then, looking round some bushy trees
Poor Willie, weeping, Rupert sees.

To him he hurries on tiptoe,
And says, "Why do you treat us so?"

"My uncle's sent a plane in bits,
But though I've tried just nothing fits."

While Bill and Rupert are talking they hear someone approaching, and soon Willie appears carrying a slender piece of wood over his shoulder. "Hi, Willie," cries Rupert, "we're both wanting to see you." But the little mouse turns and scuttles away again without a word. Rupert leaves Bill and strolls away, but as he passes some bushes he suddenly spies a little figure sitting on a bank.

He approaches so quietly that Willie doesn't suspect his presence until he is right beside him. Then the little mouse starts violently. "Oh dear," cries Willie. "I'd meant to keep it a secret until it was finished, but it's no good. You see, it's my birthday and I've had a wonderful present. My uncle has sent me an airplane in parts and I'm not strong enough to put them together."

RUPERT LENDS A HAND

Then Rupert says, "Why build in here?
You'll never get it out, I fear!"

They take the pieces all outside,
And Willie brings the plans as guide.

He thinks awhile, then says, "From here,
We can't take off, it's very clear."

Since petrol's missing from the plane,
A handle's use they ascertain.

Rupert finds the shed full of pieces of wood and metal. With much care they carry the parts out into the orchard and start to re-erect them. At length most of the little plane is built. Then a new thought strikes Rupert. "If it really flies," he says, "we should never be able to take off in your orchard. Let's move it into Farmer Brown's field; there's plenty of room there."

Leaving the partly-built plane in Farmer Brown's field, the two friends return to unpack the engine. "I didn't see any petrol tanks," says Rupert. "My uncle said that was his best invention," says Willie. "There's a wonderful lot of wheels in that case, so that when you turn the handle the propeller works without petrol."

They turn the handle, fierce wind blows,
And backwards both the youngsters throws;

With engines fixed, and blades on top,
Says Rupert, "Now we'll have a hop."

Willie leaves, but back he flies:
"The bull is charging, help!" he cries.

So in the plane they quickly hide,
The handle turn, and upward glide.

Rupert gives the handle a vigorous couple of turns. The propeller whizzes round at such a rate that the wind from it blows him right back.

The engine is very light, and the two pals soon have it in place. "Why, it's an autogyro," says Willie. "Oh," cries Rupert in great excitement, "let's see how she flies." But at the last minute Willie holds back. "I don't believe I dare go up," he quavers.

In spite of Rupert's persuasions, Willie won't venture into the little plane, and finally he walks away. Almost at once there is a shout, and he sees his small friend racing back towards him. "The bull, the bull!" screams Willie. "It's seen me and it's charging this way." Rupert clambers into the cockpit and drags the little mouse after him. The propeller whizzes round and in a moment they are off the ground.

RUPERT LANDS IN WATER

He pulls the stick to find control,
And over through a loop they roll.

"It's easy, Willie, come, you try,"
He says, but Willie cries, "Not I."

Now Rupert's arms grow tired at last;
"I cannot land," he says, aghast.

And then the breezes take a hand,
And down upon the lake they land.

Now that he is in the air Rupert suddenly feels very unsafe. "I've never worked one of these things before," he says, rather shakily. "How did I manage to get it off the ground?"

Rupert is now feeling very nervous, but the plane doesn't play any tricks. He works the handle steadily and they mount higher and higher until they are above the clouds.

Before long Rupert has other things to worry about. "I can't keep this up," he groans. "And I don't know how to land. Oh, dear, supposing we crash!" To his great relief the rotor blades keep spinning overhead so that they drop very gently. "I believe that is Nutwood Lake over there," he cries happily. Just then a gust of wind catches them and blows them straight towards the water.

RUPERT FEELS UNEASY

The Brothers Fox the airplane see;
One says, "Whatever can it be?"

But off they go to get some rope,
And Rupert fixes it in hope.

When they are safe on land again,
They start to tell about the plane.

"They're odd," thinks Rupert. "I'll decide
The handle of the plane to hide."

On the bank there is a sound of running, and two figures appear near a tree. They are the brothers, Freddy and Ferdy Fox.

Rupert and Willie are overjoyed to see someone near them, and they shout for help. The Foxes turn and disappear, but in a few moments they return with a length of rope and heave one end across the water. Rupert grabs it and ties it to a strut.

Freddy and Ferdy manage to get the little plane to the shore before it sinks. Rupert thanks them, but the Foxes don't seem interested. "We're out for a picnic," says Ferdy. "We've found a disused hut in the wood. Come and see it." As the little party walks away Rupert gets more uneasy because the brothers are well known for the tricks they play. He drops behind, runs back to the plane and hides the driving handle.

They're taken to a hut that's damp;
It seems a curious place to camp.

The door slams, someone turns the key.
"We're tricked," says Rupert. "Don't you see?"

"We must get out," poor Willie cries;
"Don't worry, now," his friend replies.

By pushing hard the thatch they lift,
And then escape is sure and swift.

Freddy and Ferdy Fox lead the way, and there, sure enough, is a hut with the door open. "It's a queer place to choose," says Rupert. On entering the hut Rupert and Willie look round. Suddenly the door slams, the key is turned and outside there is the sound of laughter. "What on earth are the Foxes up to?" asks Willie. "Why, don't you see," cries Rupert. "They have tricked us. Now that we are prisoners."

"Don't worry too much," says Rupert, quietly. He finds that the door is secure and the walls are strong. After testing the latch at several points, Rupert finds a place where it is old and loose. Eagerly he pushes it up, drops out, and then lends a back while Willie follows suit. "Thank goodness we're free again," says the little mouse. "Hush," says Rupert. "I don't want Freddy and Ferdy to know."

RUPERT FLIES AGAIN

Now Willie, nearly in despair,
Cries, "Look! They'll soon be in the air."

"Now to the plane we'll hurry back
Before," he says, "they're on our track."

"How did you know they couldn't fly?"
Asks Willie; Rupert says, "Well, I

Took out the handle from the plane.
See, here it is! We'll fly again."

Creeping silently beside a hedge, Rupert and Willie peer through it. In the field beyond is the plane. Freddy is inside while Ferdy stands near looking rather puzzled. While they crouch close to the hedge Freddy and Ferdy leave the plane and trot out of the field on their way back to the hut. "There they go," laughs Rupert. "They may be annoyed to find that we are no longer in the hut."

As they reach the plane Willie turns to Rupert. "How could you tell what the Foxes would do?" he demands. "Well, you see," grins the little bear, "when the Foxes found they couldn't fly the plane, I knew they'd go back to the hut to ask us all about it," and Rupert smilingly produces the handle from under his jersey. They scramble quickly into the plane, the handle is fitted, and in a moment they are in the air.

RUPERT
and
OZZIE

The day of the big parade is also
a great day for Rupert. He travels to the
city with his new friend to see the show
and then discovers something that goes
on secretly under the ground.

Illustrated by ALFRED BESTALL
Originally published in the *Daily Express* in 1953, the year of the Queen's Coronation!

RUPERT LOOKS IN THE ATTIC

The long-stored things that Rupert finds
Are used for games of many kinds.

Says he, "Though I can't guess them all,
Maybe I'll see the stumps and ball."

"It is almost midsummer," thinks Rupert one morning, "and I haven't had a game of cricket yet! It is time I started." So he asks his mummy if he may go up to the attic and see what he can find stored away. Mrs Bear agrees and Rupert makes his way upstairs to the room in the loft. At the door he stops in amazement. "Oo-oo! I had no idea there were so many things stored away," he exclaims. The room is packed with articles and lumber of every shape and size, but that is not all. "Why, there are lots of things that must belong to Daddy," says Rupert. "I didn't know he played so many sports and games." Rupert recognises some of the things at once, but others are so strangely shaped that they mystify him. "I will come back later on and try to guess which games the things are used for," he says to himself. "It would be a good puzzle to remember for a rainy day."

(Do you know what sports and games all these things are used for? Turn to p68 to find the answers!)

RUPERT CALLS TO DINKIE

"Please, Mummy, may I go and play?"
Asks Rupert. "It's a lovely day."

He's on his way to visit Bill
When Dinkie marches down the hill.

The cat struts by, so prim and sleek,
"But why," thinks Rupert, "won't he speak?"

So Rupert's left to stand and stare,
While Dinkie walks on, nose in air.

Then, eager to get into the fresh air, he searches about and soon discovers some stumps and a cricket ball. Pleased with his find, he hurries from the attic and asks to go and see if his pal, Bill Badger, still has a bat. Mrs Bear gives her consent and Rupert sets off by a shortcut. On his way he happens to see a black cat striding out in the opposite direction. "That's Dinkie, Beryl's cat," he murmurs. "I wonder why he is hurrying away from home." Being very inquisitive, Rupert hurries after the cat. "Hi! Where are you off to?" he calls. "Are you going hunting?" Then he pauses. "No, you can't be," he adds. "You're all dressed up with a new ribbon. Perhaps you're going to a party. Is that it?" But Dinkie walks straight on with his nose in the air and pays no attention. "Well! There's a queer thing!" gasps Rupert as the little creature disappears. "Cats are very odd. He must be on some secret journey. Why won't he tell?"

RUPERT NOTICES A STRANGER

Bill Badger, at his cottage gate,
Hears Rupert's call and turns to wait.

Upon a ridge the stranger stands;
He has a camera in his hands.

As they go past, he gives a shout,
Then starts to jump and dance about.

He follows them with bounds and leaps
And well in sight of them he keeps.

Rupert watches the silent cat until it is out of sight. Then he runs on to find his friend Bill. "Hello, do you want some cricket?" cries the little badger. "I'll get my bat and we'll have some practice on the Common." Soon they are on higher ground and Rupert is telling of the cat's puzzling behaviour when Bill interrupts. "Look, a stranger," he whispers. "He's taking photos of the villages around him. I've never seen anyone quite like him before. Who can he be?" The two friends walk past the stranger and try not to stare at him. He does not appear to notice then, but when they are part way down the next slope they hear a wild, "Coo-ee!" and see him waving. "What does he want? Must we go back?" says Rupert, nervously. Suddenly the stranger makes for them, moving forward in such tremendous leaps that they take fright and scamper as fast as they possibly can towards the thickest part of the wood.

RUPERT IS FOUND IN HIDING

They crouch in hiding on the ground,
And watch the stranger look around.

Then as they crouch amongst the trees,
Poor Rupert gives a great big sneeze.

At once the stranger sees the pair.
He asks, "Why are you hiding there?"

He says that "Ozzie" is his name,
So Bill invites him to their game.

The little friends gain the cover of some dense undergrowth before the odd-looking stranger overtakes them. They hear him leap into the wood and stop quite near them. Peeping out, they see him gazing around in a puzzled way. All at once Rupert feels a tickling in his nose. Frantically he tries to hold his breath and buries his face in his handkerchief, but he cannot prevent a loud sneeze. The newcomer turns sharply, and their hiding place is discovered. "P-please, we didn't mean to be rude by running away," Bill quavers as he and Rupert face the stranger. "But we've never seen anyone like you, Mr -er-er –" "Don't call me Mister," says the other heartily, "my name's Ozzie — short for Oswald. I've come round the world to see your beautiful homeland. They made me bring an umbrella though your weather's lovely, but my chief joy is cricket, and when I saw you two carrying cricket things I just had to follow you, hoping for a game."

RUPERT BOWLS AT THE WICKET

Shouts Ozzie, "There's the very place!"
And sets off at a rapid pace.

He finds some grassy ground that's flat,
The pals agree that he should bat.

The ball is bowled by Rupert Bear
And Ozzie taps it back with care.

But then he hits with all his might,
Which sends the ball right out of sight.

In his relief at finding the stranger friendly, Bill offers him his bat. "Would you like a game with us?" he asks timidly. "My, this is great!" cries Ozzie. "I haven't held a cricket bat for months. Come on, let's find a pitch. Whizzo!" He bounds away too fast for Rupert and Bill to keep pace, but they find him on a fairly flat part of the Common, and Rupert puts in stumps while Bill takes the umbrella to mark the bowler's end of the pitch. The little pals ask their new friend to bat first, and they mark out the pitch short enough to suit Rupert's strength. "Now let's see if my eye is as true as it used to be," says Ozzie. "My, what a rummy pitch it is!" At first he bats gently, sending each ball to where Rupert or Bill can easily field it, but at length his patience gives out, and, opening his shoulders, he swings the bat round and makes a tremendous high drive over Bill's head. The ball sails across the sky and down a distant slope.

They run to where they saw it fall,
And search about to find the ball.

"Oh, dear," says Ozzie, "I'm to blame;
To lose it now would be a shame."

They keep on searching round the slope,
Until at last they give up hope.

Then Ozzie says, "Come on, you two.
I'm sure there's something I can do."

Bill gazes in admiration as the ball disappears from sight. "What a topping hit!" he shouts. "How I wish I was strong enough to do that!" "That was marvellous. It must count six!" adds Rupert. "Quick, let's mark the spot where it went." They race over the brow. Then they pause in anxiety, for the hollow beyond it is a tangle of long grass and bushes and some rabbit holes. All three join in the search and hunt around busily, but the farther they go the more unlikely it seems that the friends will ever find the missing ball in the thick undergrowth. "Oh dear, I didn't mean this to happen," Ozzie moans. "After not playing for so long I just couldn't resist one good slog. These bushes are terrible, and we don't even know where it fell. Come, take me to your village. I must think what to do." So Rupert and Bill collect their things from the pitch and off they go. "We'll take you by a shortcut," Rupert tells their new friend.

RUPERT ASKS THE SHOPKEEPER

Along the village street they stop
When Rupert says, "Let's try this shop."

But Mr Mudge says with a sigh,
"There's not a cricket ball to buy!"

Poor Ozzie's feeling quite upset.
Says Rupert, "We may find it yet."

Back at his home, to his delight,
He's greeted by a splendid sight.

On their way down from the Common, Ozzie tells the little pals stories of his far-away country where cricket is so very important. Then he asks if the village has a sports shop which might sell cricket balls. "Why, yes," cries Rupert. "Here's Mr Mudge's, that's a sort of sports shop. At any rate, he sells Snap and Ludo, as well as sweets and collar studs." But inside the shop Mr Mudge shakes his head. "I haven't a cricket ball left," he murmurs. Out in the street, Ozzie gets more and more gloomy, and Rupert tries to cheer him up. "It doesn't really matter," he says. "My ball was very old and, anyway, we may find it yet." But Ozzie won't be comforted. "I must make it up to you somehow," he says. "So let me write down your address. Then I can call on you." When they separate, Rupert goes home and finds his daddy busily hanging coloured flags between his cottage and the hedge. "They do look fine," thinks the little bear.

RUPERT HANGS UP SOME FLAGS

While Rupert hangs the flags around,
He hears a pop-pop-popping sound.

The car swings slowly round the bend,
And driving it he sees his friends.

"Why, Ozzie," Rupert cries in glee.
"Perhaps you'd like to stay to tea."

Says Ozzie, "Please, may Rupert go
With me to see tomorrow's show?"

"Come on, Rupert," says Mr Bear. "You're just in time to help me brighten the place up with these flags. We must be as gay as we can to celebrate the great things that are going to happen." Rupert agrees happily and while he works, he tells all about the new friend he has met. After an hour or so he hears an odd noise. A moment later an astonishing old car pulls up beside the hedge and seated at the wheel is Ozzie himself. Getting down from the steps, Rupert runs to the gate to meet his new friend and to introduce him. Mrs Bear asks him into the cottage and soon Ozzie is joining the family at tea. "I want to give the little bear a treat," he says, "to make amends for losing his ball. What I've really come to this country for is to see the wonderful procession in the great city. May I take Rupert to see it too?" At that Rupert's eyes sparkle with excitement and he turns hopefully to his mummy and daddy. "Oh, please may I go?" he implores.

RUPERT BEGINS A LONG TRIP

"I'll come back later on today,"
Calls Ozzie as he drives away.

"Now here's a flag," says Mrs Bear,
"But please be good and do take care."

That evening Ozzie calls again;
His car is waiting in the lane.

The car chugs on, mile after mile,
And Rupert falls asleep meanwhile.

Mr and Mrs Bear are taken by surprise at Ozzie's idea, and they think carefully. "Well, I never expected Rupert would get such a chance," says Mrs Bear at length. "You'll promise to take good care of him, won't you?" Ozzie promises earnestly, and after giving the necessary instructions he chugs away in his funny little car. "You will need a flag to wave," says Mrs Bear when she has gone indoors. "Here is just the thing." As the time for Rupert's departure draws near Mrs Bear becomes more and more anxious, for Ozzie had decided to start late in the evening and drive through the night. But she has given her word, and making sure that Rupert has lots of sandwiches, she sees him off. "This is the only car I could hire round here," says Ozzie. "Let's hope it holds out." The old thing rattles and clatters through the darkness but, in spite of that, Rupert keeps himself warm with a travelling rug and sleeps soundly for most of the journey.

RUPERT STARES AT THE CROWD

They reach the city streets at last,
And Ozzie makes the car doors fast.

But Ozzie's hopes begin to fade.
Such crowds await the big parade.

He says, "Let's eat our food up now.
We'll try to see the show somehow."

Then Ozzie lifts his friend up high
To watch the Queen go riding by.

Early next morning when it is hardly light, Rupert wakes to find that the little car has stopped in the quiet of a city back street. "It's very warm although it is so early," says Ozzie. "We shan't need our overcoats or gloves. Let's leave them under the seat." He pulls up the hood and makes everything secure. Then he hurries Rupert along the streets so as to get front place for the procession, but on arrival he has a shock, for the pavements are already full. "These people must have slept here all night," gasps Ozzie. "Never mind, we'll see over them." Spreading his rug, he sits down and makes a good meal while Rupert starts on Mrs Bear's sandwiches. Now there is increasing movement around them, and from the distance come noises of music and cheering. Lifting Rupert on his shoulder, Ozzie bounces up and down. The bands and the gorgeous uniforms draw near, and everybody waves and shouts, "There she is! The Queen! The Queen!"

RUPERT CLINGS TO A BRANCH

But as the crowds all cheer and sway,
The little bear is whisked away.

A stranger puts him on the ground,
And says, "There, now you're safe and sound."

Then Ozzie's penknife Rupert sees,
While all the people past him squeeze.

As homeward bound the people rush,
They carry Rupert in the crush.

For a time the cheering and the excitement are tremendous. By standing on tiptoe, Ozzie makes himself very tall, so that he and Rupert have a perfect view. At last the great procession is over, the crowds press and sway, and the little bear finds his perch on Ozzie's shoulder not so safe. All at once, feeling himself over-balancing, he drops his flag and grabs at an overhead branch until a friendly stranger takes his weight and sets him on the ground. Rupert is alarmed to be surrounded by so many people all much taller than himself and tries to thread his way through in different directions. "I *must* find Ozzie," he thinks. "He can't be far off." Suddenly something on the ground catches his eyes, and he picks it up. "Why, that's Ozzie's pocket knife," he murmurs. "I saw him use it on his sandwiches. I must be going towards him." So he moves on until he feels himself being carried along by the sightseers as they surge through an opening and down some steps.

RUPERT WATCHES THE MOUSE

Some steps appear, he starts to glide.
It seems the strangest kind of ride!

He wriggles from the crowd at last,
And watches all the feet go past.

"I'm tired," says Rupert with a sigh.
And then he sees a mouse nearby.

"Pssst! Follow me," the creature calls,
And through a little hole it crawls.

Rupert tries to turn and push his way back up the steps, but the crowd is too thick. He is swept along into a large hall where people seem to be swirling in all directions. "There's lots of them going another way. I'll join them; they may be going out," he thinks. But to his dismay he finds himself on a moving staircase being carried further downwards. At the bottom he topples over and manages to dodge out of their way. "If I stay here I may yet see Ozzie," he mutters. The endless stream of people surges past Rupert until he gets quite dizzy from looking at them, and still there is no sign of Ozzie. "Oh dear, I'll never get home from here," he moans, sinking down wearily. Gradually he becomes aware that a bright pair of eyes is watching him from the shadows and, turning, he spies a large mouse. "Pssst, come this way!" says the creature mysteriously. Next instant it has flicked out of sight down a hole, leaving Rupert staring in surprise.

RUPERT IS TOLD TO FOLLOW

As Rupert kneels upon the floor,
A panel slides back like a door.

The little bear stares in surprise,
"Quick, come inside," his mouse friend cries.

The mouse says, "Listen to my plan,
I mean to help you if I can.

Come down these steps and you will see.
Don't lag behind. Just keep with me."

The mouse has appeared and vanished so suddenly that the little bear wonders if he has been imagining things. While he waits with a puzzled frown there is a click, and a panel in the wall slides back revealing a dark space beyond. Peering inside, Rupert sees a mass of machinery with its wheels spinning silently and just below, on a rough step, is the mouse. "Hurry up. Come on in and let's shut the panel again," says the tiny creature urgently. When the panel is shut Rupert waits to get used to the dim light. "And now what are you moaning about?" demands the mouse. "You look nicer than those humans out there. Perhaps I can help you." "Well, if I've lost my big pal Ozzie, and I want to get home to Nutwood," sighs Rupert. "I can't find your pal in that crowd," says the mouse, "but I can get you home. It's lucky you've met me!" And he leads the way down the rough staircase. "I hope he is not playing a joke on me," thinks Rupert.

RUPERT HURTLES DOWN A SLIDE

Such heavy rumblings Rupert hears;
A moving staircase then appears.

Those stairs go flat beneath his treat,
And rapidly he shoots ahead.

The journey down is very fast,
But Rupert sees the end at last.

"Ha, ha!" the mouse laughs. "How was that?"
As Rupert gets up from the mat.

After going down many steps the flight bends to the left. "My goodness! There's another moving staircase!" cries Rupert. "Yes, get onto it carefully. It's not going too fast," says the mouse. "And mind you don't touch any of the machinery." The little creature scampers on ahead and Rupert, obeying orders, tries to follow, but hardly has he set food on the moving staircase when the whole thing flattens out and becomes a slide. "Whatever's happening? This is awful! I can't stop!" he

gasps. On he goes, faster and faster until he is quite breathless. "Oh dear, I shall land with a terrible bump!" he thinks. Next moment he is shot off onto a series of mats at the bottom of the staircase and turns three somersaults before he can stop. "Ha, ha! That was lovely," says a happy little voice. The mouse has watched his antics with glee. "What an awful place!" gasps Rupert. "You shouldn't call a place awful just because it's strange to you!" says the mouse.

RUPERT ENTERS A DARK TUNNEL

While Rupert rests, his friend explains,
"Down here we have a lot of trains!"

"I can't see any," Rupert cries.
"Then come with me," the mouse replies.

Right through the tunnel track they go
To where some engines puff and blow.

The tunnel's brighter round the bend,
And there they see the mouse's friend.

While Rupert is sitting and trying to recover his breath the mouse starts to explain. "When I first found you, you were in what those human beings call the Underground Railway," he says. "Stupid creatures! Their railway only goes a few miles. Now our railway will take you anywhere in the country!" "This doesn't look like a railway," quavers Rupert. "How does it work?" "Come and see!" cries the mouse. Then he turns very swiftly and runs down a dark, steamy tunnel. At the end of the tunnel Rupert gazes in at more engines and more wheels whizzing round with no sound except the hiss of steam. "There, isn't this lovely!" says the mouse. "That's what drives our railway, nobody knows why. Even the Imps' back-room boys who made it have forgotten how it works!" "I hope it won't break down!" says Rupert nervously. "Don't worry, it never goes wrong," declares the mouse, as he leads Rupert into a brighter tunnel where someone is working.

RUPERT MEETS OLD MR MOLE

*"Please, Rupert wants to find a train
To take him straight back home again."*

*"H'm," Mr Mole says, "I'll assist.
Just let me check my special list."*

*"I know which one now," he exclaims,
Then shuffles past the station names.*

*He opens up the Nutwood door,
And says, "You'll soon be home once more."*

The stranger turns as Rupert approaches and the mouse introduces him. "This is Mr Mole. He's the new stationmaster here, so he can take charge of you now. And this," he adds, turning to Mr Mole, "is Rupert Bear — he wants to get to Nutwood." "H'm! Never seen you on our railway before. And there are not many wanting to go to Nutwood. Let's see, that's on the Nutchester line, isn't it?" says Mr Mole. "My memory isn't what it was. I'd better jot it down." And he peers at a list on the wall. After writing some directions for himself on a piece of paper, Mr Mole shuffles down a long corridor. "Oo, look at all these doors," cries Rupert. Mr Mole says nothing until he spies the word Nutwood on one of the boards. Then he clicks the door open. "There you are. In you go, little bear. This is a quick one to Nutwood — first stop." "It looks awfully dark. Where's the train?" whispers Rupert. "Go on in," says the mouse.

RUPERT HAS A BUMPY JOURNEY

"Don't worry, you'll be quite all right,"
He adds. "Just press that bottom light."

At once the floor begins to jump,
And down goes Rupert with a bump!

He's thrown and tossed along at speed,
The journey home is rough indeed!

At last he feels the carpet dip,
He gasps, "I shan't forget this trip!"

"What shall I do now?" asks Rupert as he enters the tunnel. "And what are those three lights on the panel?" "You'll soon find out," says Mr Mole, "if you'll press the bottom light." "And now, goodbye," calls the mouse. Rupert puts his finger on the lowest light just as Mr Mole shuts the door with a clang. At the same moment something queer happens to the floor. Rupert's feet are flicked from under him and down he goes with a bump. The little bear is so surprised and

dazed that he hardly notices that the tunnel is now flooded with light. He is being tossed about and shaken uncomfortably, but at length he manages to struggle back to a sitting position. "Why, this isn't a moving staircase. It's a moving floor!" he gasps. "Oh my, how bumpy it is!" On and on he goes, faster and faster for mile after mile, and Rupert finds it hard to stay upright at such speed. The moving carpet suddenly dips downward and he is flung off onto yet another mat.

RUPERT OPENS THE TRAPDOOR

A painted arrow shows the way.
"It's Nutwood," Rupert thinks. "Hooray!"

He climbs the steps without a stop,
Until at last he's at the top.

The trapdoor rises as he winds;
It leads up to a lane, he finds.

Then Rupert's startled by a clang!
The lid has dropped down with a bang.

Once more Rupert turns a couple of somersaults before sitting up breathlessly. "Oh dear, I do wish this journey would finish," he whispers. "Hello, there's a sign saying 'Way Out'. I hope there are no more moving stairways." Following the arrow, he climbs rough steps and finds his way barred by an iron trapdoor too heavy for him to push open. "There's a little handle here," he murmurs. "I'd better give it a turn, and see what happens." Rupert finds the handle stiff to turn, but to

his delight it does the trick, the trapdoor opens and he puts his head out into the sunshine. Then he gives a shout of joy. "This is Nutwood. It's my own village!" As he scrambles out there is a whirring and a clicking and he just moves clear as the flap shuts with a bang. "My, that was dangerous!" he thinks. "I've often wondered what those iron things in the road were. Now I know! But I don't suppose many people do. I must tell Mummy about it."

Says PC Growler, "Rupert Bear,
We've all been searching everywhere!"

"Come on," he says,"We'd better go.
We all thought you were lost, you know."

Soon Rupert's mummy comes in sight.
He runs and holds her very tight.

He then explains where he has been,
And all about the things he's seen.

Hearing Rupert's shout and the noise of the trapdoor shutting, Constable Growler hurries round the corner and stares in amazement. "Why, where have you been?" he cries. "There's been a telephone call from Mr Ozzie in the big city saying that you were lost. He sounded terribly upset – and now everyone here is worrying about you!" Rupert tries to tell him about the procession and the crowds, but the constable takes his hand and marches him homeward as fast as he can.

Before he reaches his cottage, Rupert spies Mrs Bear coming towards him and, breaking away from Constable Growler, he goes to meet her. Soon all is happiness. "I'll go and spread the news that he's back," says the constable. When he has reached his home, Rupert sits down to a good tea and tells all about his outing and about Mr Mole. "I do wish I could let Ozzie know that I am safe," he says. "He must be very anxious about me. If only I knew where to find him."

RUPERT LISTENS TO THE CAT

Says Rupert Bear when morning comes,
"I'd like to go and find my chums."

Across the fields he starts to scout,
To see if anyone is out.

Then in the distance, Rupert sees
A small black creature by the trees.

He asks the cat, "Where have you been?"
And Dinkie says, "To see the Queen!"

After the excitement of the day Rupert goes to bed early. He sleeps long and soundly, and next morning he rises fresh and cheerful with no bruises from his bumpy journey. "Please may I go out?" he asks. "My pals must hear all about my adventure, but first I want to see if I can find my ball among the bushes where Ozzie hit it. I may forget where the place is." Mrs Bear gives her consent and, leaving off his scarf again because the day is hot, he scampers away over the Common. Before he reaches the tangle of bushes, Rupert sees a small black creature moving very wearily and painfully near them. "Why, that's Dinkie!" he murmurs. "How tired he looks. I wonder if he is still too proud to speak to me." He moves across and Dinkie sits and waits for him. "Hello," Rupert calls. "You've lost your beautiful bow. Have you had an adventure like me? I've been to the city and ..." "What! You too?" says Dinkie. "How did you get back so soon?"

RUPERT TELLS HIS ADVENTURES

"I saw the great procession too,"
Says Rupert. "Then what did you do?"

"I just walked home," the cat replies.
"And now I feel so tired," he sighs.

To find the lost ball Rupert turns,
But Dunkie knows the spot, he learns.

"It's in those bushes," says the cat.
And Rupert murmurs, "Fancy that!"

Something in Dinkie's voice makes Rupert more inquisitive. "I believe you have had an adventure," he says. "Come, tell me, Pussy Cat, Pussy Cat, where have you been?" "I've been up to London to see the Queen." "And what did you do when you got there?" "I nearly got trodden on everywhere!" "So did I!" cries Rupert. "We may have been in the same crowd. Did you come back by Mr Mole's Underground Railway too?" "No, I walked all the way – both ways!" sighs the cat. Seeing that Dinkie is so tired, Rupert moves off. "Well, I expect you want to get home," he says. "I'm looking for a ball that we lost when we played with Mr Ozzie." "What sort of ball? Was it a cricket ball?" asks the cat. "If so, I saw it as I came through the bushes. Wait and I'll show you." Leading the way back for a short distance, Dinkie pauses beside a bush with thick leaves and there Rupert spies his precious ball.

RUPERT REMEMBERS THE CAR

Then Dinkie sinks down quite forlorn;
He feels so weary and so worn.

"Don't worry – I know what to do,"
Says Rupert. "I will carry you!"

So through the fields he starts to run,
And says, "Your journey's nearly done."

But when he stops outside his door,
He sees friend Ozzie's car once more.

Rupert is delighted to recover his ball and, turning for home, he begins prattling merrily away about his recent adventure, but all at once he realises that he is talking to himself. Dinkie is no longer with him, but is sitting, quite exhausted, in the long grass. "Oh, you poor thing!" exclaims the little bear. "You're worn out with your tremendous walk. You must let me help you. I know, I'll carry you home." And pocketing his ball, he lifts the cat in his arms and it is soon purring.

On his way home Rupert tells the cat all about Mr Mole's railway. "You could never have come that way," he laughs. "It was a mouse who showed me into it and he would have run away from you!" Suddenly he breaks into a trot as something on the road below catches his eye. Running to the cottage he finds a strange object standing outside it. "Whose is that old car?" asks Dinkie. "Ozzie's," says Rupert. "He has come back. I must go in and find him."

RUPERT HAS OZZIE'S PENKNIFE

As Rupert goes indoors he hears
Poor Ozzie telling of his fears.

"You're not lost, Rupert! I'm so glad!"
Gasps Ozzie. "What a fright I had!"

"I've brought your things back in the car.
Just look," says Ozzie. "Here they are!"

"Yes, I've got something here for you,"
Smiles Rupert. "Here's your penknife too!"

Inside the cottage Ozzie is pouring out his troubles and trying to explain how he lost Rupert in the swaying crowd after the procession. To his surprise Mrs Bear does not seem at all worried. She is even smiling. As Ozzie pauses the door opens and in rushes Rupert himself! Ozzie can hardly believe his eyes as he snatches up the little bear and puts him on a chair. "Well, this beats everything!" he gasps. "Yes, I came home on the Underground, the real Underground,"

Rupert laughs. When he has got over the shock of seeing Rupert safe and sound, Ozzie goes to his car. "Look, I've brought your coat and your flag. They're safe too," he cries. Then Mrs Bear makes some tea and gives Dinkie a saucer of milk, and Rupert has the chance to tell again his strange adventure with the mouse and Mr Mole. "And here's something I nearly forgot," he adds. "I picked it up in that crowd." And from his pocket he takes Ozzie's penknife.

RUPERT'S LOST PROPERTY

Oh dear! Rupert is lost in the great city.

Follow the co-ordinates below and colour in the squares
to reveal something else that has gone missing.
The first square – B3 – has been coloured for you.
You could use different coloured pens for each square!

Answer on page 68.

Colour in:

B3	L7	Q4	T7
E3	L6	Q3	T8
C3	J8	O5	S6
B8	I8	O7	O6
C6	L3	T3	S8
D3	L4	O3	S3
B7	R8	O4	H8
G4	B4	B5	B6
G5	G6	G7	G8
M3	M6	N3	N6
Q6	Q7	Q8	R3
G3	L8	Q5	U6
D6	L5	O8	T6

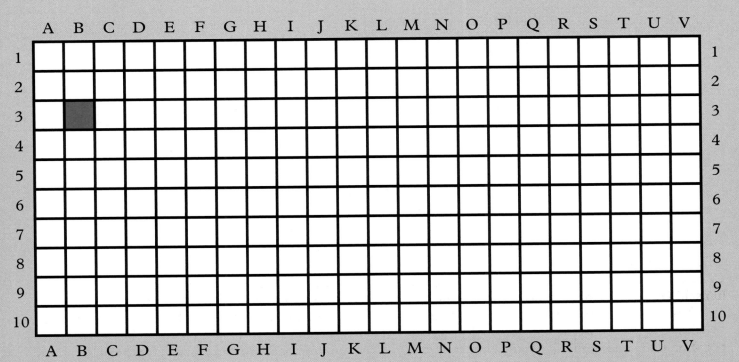

RUPERT AND THE WONDER MACHINE

THE OLD PROFESSOR always has a fresh surprise for Rupert and his chums. One day they find him trying out a strange gadget with two rollers. "Whatever is it?" asks Rex Rabbit. "It looks like my mummy's wringer, but much smaller!"

The Professor smiles and puts a piece of plain paper between the rollers, then he winds it into the machine. As he does so, Rupert exclaims, "Why! It's coming out with my name written on it!"

"That's what it appears to do," chuckles the Professor. "But it's really a trick. I call it my Wonder Machine. I'll show you how it's made."

Ask an adult to help.

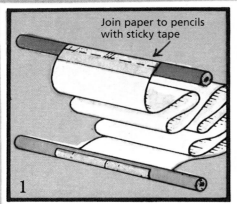

1 — Join paper to pencils with sticky tape

2 — Turn pencils as shown to wind paper

3 — Holder: 18.8cm x 4.6cm. Cut slots. 5cm — 8.8cm — 5cm. Bend sides of holder. Shape of bracket. Cut 4.

The Professor's gadget is very easy to make. Cut some strips of thin paper 7.6cm wide and join them with glue or sticky tape to make a piece about 1m 7cm long. Fix a round, unsharpened pencil to each end (Figure 1). Wind the long strip onto the pencils, turning them as shown until you have roughly an equal amount of paper on each (Figure 2). Make the holder out of stiff card (not too thick). Cut it to the size in Figure 3 with slots just wide enough to take the pencil ends. Bend the ho on the score lines and turn up the sides. Make four corner brackets, but do not fix them yet.

4 — Place pencils in slots and loop elastic band over ends

5 — Glue bracket at each corner

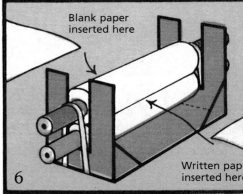

6 — Blank paper inserted here. Written pap inserted her

Drop the ends of the pencils into the slots. Keep the rollers firmly wound and slip a long rubber band over the ends of the pencils, taking it under the holder (Figure 4). Glue a bracket to each corner of the holder (Figure 5). Your Wonder Machine is now made. Cut two slips of thin paper, 7.6cm wide, and write your name on one piece, then feed it between the rollers by turning one of the pencils, until it just disappears into the machine. Now feed the blank slip into the opposite side by turning the other pencil. As the blank paper goes in, so it w seem to come out the other side with your name on it! Practise a few times with the machine, then you will be rea to baffle your chums!

This is how the Professor prepares the plans of things he invents. No one could tell what it is without knowing the secret. So take a pencil and carefully draw along all the blue and yellow lines, leaving the other colours untouched. What have you drawn?

Originally published in the *Rupert Annual* in 1977. Artist uncredited on original artwork.

Answer on page 68.

REDIRECTED POST

No wonder the postmen couldn't deliver these letters!
Can you work out who they are for?
Answers on page 68.

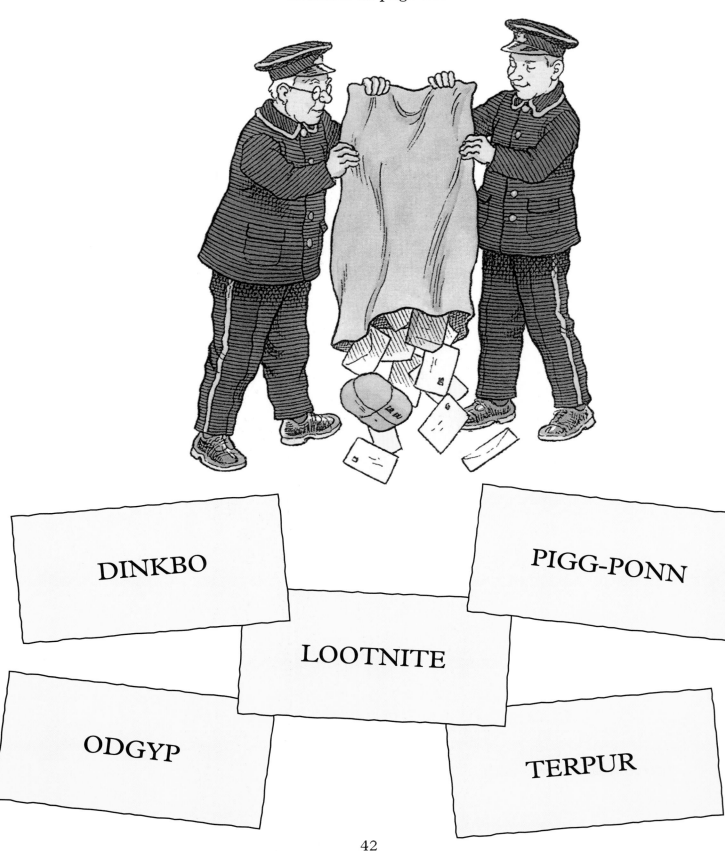

DINKBO

PIGG-PONN

LOOTNITE

ODGYP

TERPUR

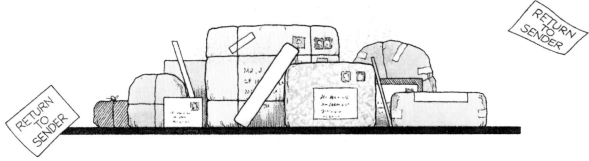

RUPERT
and the
Mail Train

Illustrated by JOHN HARROLD
Originally published in the *Daily Express* in 1994

RUPERT'S MOTHER PLANS A TRIP

Rupert goes shopping with his mum.
The pair wait for their bus to come …

"To get to Nutchester we'll need
To catch a train next — the High Speed!"

"The train's just leaving! We're too late!
I don't suppose they'll make it wait …"

"Don't worry! There's another train,"
The clerk says when the pair explain.

One autumn morning Rupert and his mother decide to go into Nutchester to visit the shops. "We'll make an early start," says Mrs Bear. "I want to be there before it gets too crowded …" Rupert enjoys going on his mother's shopping expeditions as they normally travel to Nutchester by train. "Here's the bus for the station!" he calls excitedly. As they drive off, Mrs Bear looks up the times of Nutchester trains. "That's good!" she says. "The next one's almost due."

When they arrive at the station, Rupert and his mother are dismayed to see that the train is already leaving. "We haven't even got tickets yet!" says Mrs Bear. "I suppose we'll just have to catch the next one …" "Nutchester?" says the ticket clerk. "No need to worry! There should be another train along in a few minutes' time. The one you missed was running late. I'll give you your tickets and you can wait on the platform until it comes. Nutchester will be the first stop."

Soon, as they wait, the travellers see
A train approaching rapidly …

"Climb in!" says Mrs Bear. "There's two
Free seats together that will do."

The other passenger inside
Their carriage sleeps throughout the ride.

Then Mrs Bear gasps in dismay.
"We're travelling a different way!"

Sure enough, Rupert soon spots a train approaching the station. "This must be the one!" says Mrs Bear. "We'll wait for it to stop, then look for an empty carriage." To their surprise, the train is already quite crowded. "That's odd!" says Rupert's mother. "Perhaps it's Market Day? People must have travelled in from outlying villages." "I hope there are enough seats left for us!" says Rupert. "Yes," smiles Mrs Bear. "Here are two together. Let's climb in …"

The only other passenger in the Bears' carriage is a postman, who is sound asleep. "He probably had an early start," says Rupert's mother. "In Nutwood, the post arrives before we've even finished breakfast!" Rupert gazes happily at the scenery as the train speeds along. Suddenly, the carriage gives a lurch and veers off along another line. "Oh dear!" says Mrs Bear. "I'm sure this can't be right. *That* looks like the way to Nutchester, so where can we be going?"

The postman wakes – amazed to see
He suddenly has company …

"This train's not meant for folk like you!
It only stops at our H.Q.!"

The train speeds on till Rupert sees
A building peeping through the trees.

"All change!" a voice begins to shout
As groups of postmen clamber out.

As Mrs Bear peers anxiously out of the window the sleeping postman wakes with a start. "Hello!" he yawns. "Must have nodded off! Have we reached Nutwood yet?" "Yes," says Rupert. "That's where we got on —" "— intending to go to Nutchester," explains Mrs Bear. "Dear me!" smiles the postman. "I'm afraid you're heading the wrong way! This is the Mail Train, you see. It only stops at Postal Headquarters after Nutwood. We're on a special branch line."

The train speeds on, then finally slows to a halt. All Rupert can see is a large building, like some sort of castle … "Postal Headquarters!" calls a voice. "All change!" Stepping onto the platform, Rupert and his mother find themselves completely surrounded by postmen. Some start unloading sacks of mail, while others wheel bright red bicycles across the station yard. "Goodness!" blinks Mrs Bear. "I'd no idea our letters came here! I wonder when the train goes back?"

RUPERT JOINS THE OTHERS

The friendly postman says he'll show
The visitors the way to go …

"The Postmaster can tell you when
The Nutwood train sets out again."

Rupert knocks at a bright red door.
"Come in!" a voice calls. "Join the tour!"

"Follow the others, please. This way!
We'll start off now, without delay …"

In the bustle of the crowd, Rupert spots the friendly postman who shared their carriage. "I'm not sure about trains back to Nutwood," he says. "The best place to ask is at Head Office. Come with me and I'll show you where it is." Leading the way to the large building Rupert saw earlier, the postman points towards a red door. "Ask for the Postmaster," he calls. "He'll sort something out. I'd come with you, if I wasn't on duty, but I'm afraid I have to go and join the sorting …"

Rupert knocks at the red door. "Come in!" calls a loud voice. Inside, a group of young postmen are being shown a plan of the building by the Postmaster. "This is where training starts," he declares. "Arrivals and Sorting. Join the others, please. The tour's about to leave!" Before Mrs Bear can say anything, everyone jumps to their feet and starts marching to the door. "Bit small for a postman!" declares the old man, looking at Rupert. "Still, we'll give him a chance …"

RUPERT SEES THE SORTING OFFICE

*"The sacks you see are full of post
That has been sent from coast to coast!"*

*"It all needs sorting out, you see,
Then sent on for delivery ..."*

*"Remarkable!" blinks Mrs Bear
As postmen hurry everywhere.*

*Next moment, Rupert catches sight
Of huge airships and planes in flight ...*

Striding out of the room, the Postmaster leads Rupert and his mother along a corridor to join the other recruits. "Main Reception!" he cries. "This is where all the post arrives and is sent down to Sorting. Four deliveries a day. Comes from all over the world!" By this time, Rupert and Mrs Bear are too fascinated to interrupt, and follow the tour downstairs. "Sorting Office!" says their guide. "Letters, parcels, airmail. All filed by destination, then sent on their way."

As they follow the tour of Postal Headquarters, Rupert and his mother are astonished to see how letters and parcels are sent speeding along. "All at the double!" declares the Postmaster. "The faster, the better!" Marching briskly forward, he climbs a flight of steps and tells the new recruits to follow closely. Rupert is just about to join them when he sees an open doorway, with blue sky beyond. "Airmail!" explains a postman. "Flights are leaving all day long. It's a wonderful sight ..."

RUPERT SLIDES DOWN A CHUTE

The Postmaster explains that they
Have flights arrive and leave all day.

"I'll climb up for a better view!"
Thinks Rupert. "Then I'll see them too."

But, suddenly, he feels the wall
Behind him move, and starts to fall!

"Help!" Rupert cries. "I can't get out!"
But nobody can hear him shout …

Hurrying after the others, Rupert finds himself in a busy control tower, looking out over an airfield. "We can keep track of everything that comes and goes from up here!" declares the Postmaster proudly. "Outward post gets Top Priority." Rupert is fascinated by the special airships and clambers onto a nearby ledge to get a better view. "Runs like clockwork!" the Postmaster says. "Pilots know exactly where they're going and *we* know exactly where they are."

Marvelling at the airships, Rupert hears the Postmaster tell the new recruits how many flights they make each day. Suddenly, he feels the wall behind him starting to move. "Help!" he gasps, losing his balance … Before anyone can move, Rupert tumbles head over heels down a smooth, steep chute, which seems to go on forever! As the door above closes, he is plunged into darkness, not knowing which way is up or down. "Oh, no!" he groans. "I hope I reach the bottom soon!"

RUPERT IS REDIRECTED

*He lands, at last, with such a bump
He makes a nearby postman jump.*

*"What's this? No label! I don't know!
No one can tell where it should go!"*

*"Help!" Rupert calls out. "Stop the belt!"
But on it trundles, at full pelt.*

*He topples off the belt at last
And waits for someone to come past.*

At last Rupert spots a glimmer of light at the end of the chute. He lands with a bump in a huge jumble of parcels. "Bless me!" cries a startled postman. "This one's not even wrapped! No paper, no string and no sign of any address!" Poor Rupert is too shocked to speak as he's lifted clear of the parcels and put on a conveyor belt marked, 'Redirected Mail'. "They'll know what to do with it!" shrugs the postman. "I suppose the original label must have fallen off …"

The conveyor belt carries Rupert forward, past sacks of sorted mail. He tries calling for help but everyone is too busy to notice. "I don't suppose they can hear above the clatter!" he sighs. "It's going too fast to jump off, so I suppose I'd better just stay here and see what happens next!" The ride ends quite suddenly, with all the redirected post being tipped into a large bucket. "Thank goodness!" thinks Rupert. "As soon as someone comes I'll tell them what's happened …"

RUPERT EXPLAINS AT LAST

But then the basket starts to sway
And Rupert finds he's wheeled away!

Another postman lifts him clear.
"Well, well!" he murmurs. "What's this here?"

"I'm not a parcel!" Rupert cries.
The postman blinks in stunned surprise.

As Rupert tells the way he fell
The Postmaster arrives as well.

Just as Rupert sits up, the basket full of redirected post begins to move. "Wait!" he calls, as a postman tows it away. "I'm not a parcel!" To his dismay, the postman doesn't even look round, but simply leaves the basket and hurries on his way. "*He* didn't hear me either!" groans Rupert. At that moment a new postman starts to sort through the basket of post. "A walking bear!" he smiles as Rupert struggles to get free. "Fancy sending it through the post without a label …"

Lifting Rupert onto a workbench, the postman reaches for a sticky label marked, 'Return to Sender'. "You don't have to redirect me!" cries Rupert. "I've never been posted to start with!" "Not posted?" blinks the postman. "Then why were you in my basket?" "All an unfortunate accident!" booms the Postmaster as he strides towards the bench. "You led us quite a chase there, young man! Nearly ended up being delivered to your own house! No harm done, I'm glad to see!"

RUPERT HAS AN IDEA

*"Thank goodness!" Mrs Bear cries. "We
Had no idea where you could be!"*

*"Trains back to Nutwood leave … oh, dear!
You've missed the last train back from here!"*

*"The airships that we saw! Do they
Pass over Nutwood on the way?"*

*"They might! Let's go and ask the crew
Exactly where they're flying to …"*

"Thank goodness you're safe!" cries Mrs Bear. "I was worried when you suddenly disappeared!" "Sorry!" says Rupert. "At least I saw the Sorting Office …" "Your mother told me how you came to be here!" says the Postmaster. "It shouldn't be too difficult to get home. All you have to do is catch the next train to Nutwood …" Unfolding a timetable, he reads through a list of destinations, then shakes his head in disbelief. "Can't be done!" he blinks. "The last train has already left!"

How can Rupert and his mother get back from Postal Headquarters now that they've missed the train? Thinking hard for a moment, he suddenly remembers all the airships he saw and asks the Postmaster if any of them ever fly over Nutwood. "Good idea!" says the old man. "We don't normally take passengers but this is an emergency! The last flights of the day should still be loading up. If we look lively we'll be able to see where they're going …"

RUPERT TAKES OFF

"*Please keep the final airship moored;*
Two passengers to come aboard!"

The pilot soon agrees to wait.
"*But not for long or we'll be late!*"

"*Farewell! I hope you and your son*
Enjoy the flight. It should be fun!"

The airship takes off silently
Then gathers speed quite rapidly ...

Hurrying out to the courtyard, Rupert is dismayed to see that most of the airships have already left. "Wait!" calls the Postmaster. "Special consignment to go on the last flight!" The postman in charge leads them to a large balloon that is still being loaded with sacks of mail. "Just in time!" he cries. "A moment later and they'd have left too. It's a long-distance flight, to Greenland and the North Pole." Waving to the pilot, he tells the others to follow him straightaway.

When they reach the airship, the pilot agrees to make a special detour over Nutwood. "Thank you for sorting everything out!" Rupert's mother tells the Postmaster. "I don't know what we'd have done without you ..." "Don't mention it!" he smiles. "Always glad to be of service." Without further ado, the huge airship rises into the sky, with Rupert peering excitedly through the cabin window. The propeller starts and they glide off, away from Postal Headquarters, across the open fields ...

"Look!" Mrs Bear calls. "Down below!
There's somewhere there I think I know ..."

"It must be Nutwood!" Rupert cries.
"Yes! Buildings that I recognise!"

"Because we're on a non-stop route
I'd like you both to parachute ..."

"It's very safe. Jump when you see
Exactly where you'd like to be."

"This is wonderful!" gasps Mrs Bear. "We're gliding along with hardly a sound." Down below, Rupert can see fields and hedges, spread out like a giant map with model trees and houses. "You were lucky to catch us!" says the pilot. "Our timetable doesn't leave much room for extra stops. We normally fly north of Nutwood then out to sea. Makes a nice change to see a bit of countryside ..." "Look!" cries Rupert. "There's Nutwood now! I can recognise the church tower."

As the airship hovers over Nutwood, the co-pilot asks Rupert and Mrs Bear to come into the hold. "There isn't time for us to land," he explains. "You'll have to make a parachute jump." "Super!" cries Rupert. "Are you sure it's safe?" asks his mother. "Absolutely!" smiles the pilot. "Strap these on and I'll show you what to do." When the pair are ready, he opens a hatch and points to the village below. "When you see your house, just jump out and the parachutes will open."

RUPERT AMAZES HIS FATHER

"There's our house now!" calls Mrs Bear.
She jumps and floats down through the air.

As Rupert follows her he peers
Down at the road. "There's Dad!" he cheers.

"Great Scott!" he blinks as they drift down.
"I thought you'd both gone into town!"

"Don't tell me you flew there by plane?"
"No!" Rupert laughs. "We caught a train!"

"There's our house!" calls Mrs Bear. "I suppose we'd better jump …" Rupert follows her out of the hatch and finds himself drifting gently down as the parachute billows out above his head. "How extraordinary!" gasps Mrs Bear. "I'm flying over Nutwood like a bird!" "Wonderful!" calls Rupert. "We're going to land right in the front garden!" As they drift lower, he lets out a whoop of surprise. "There's Daddy!" he cries. "I can see him walking home along the path!"

Mr Bear can hardly believe his eyes. "Hello!" calls Rupert. "We saw you as we were coming down!" "Coming down?" blinks his father. "Where from? Why are you both wearing parachutes?" "Nothing to worry about, dear!" laughs Mrs Bear. "Rupert and I went on a journey to Nutchester …" "By aeroplane?" blinks Mr Bear. "By train!" laughs Rupert. "We only came *back* by plane! Come inside and I'll tell you all about it …"

RUPERT
and
Robo

Illustrated by STUART TROTTER

RUPERT SETS OUT TO PLAY

*Says PC Growler, "Please, watch out,
There is a burglar round about!"*

*"A robber's on the loose today?
Perhaps I won't go out to play."*

*But Mummy's keen that Rupert spends
The afternoon with all his friends.*

*So Rupert, Algy, Bill and all
Agree to meet and play some ball.*

It is the last day of the school holidays, and Rupert has been awake since dawn, helping his father around the garden. Rupert is about to oil the squeaky garden gate when PC Growler draws up. The policeman looks terribly worried, and Mr Bear asks him what the matter is.

"There's a burglar on the loose," he warns the Bears. "I would keep all your windows and doors closed if I were you."

"I was going to invite my pals for a game of football on the Common," sighs Rupert as he traipses inside to warn his mother. "Perhaps we shouldn't go."

But Mummy thinks Rupert should have fun on his last day of holiday. "Go and play," she persuades him. "We'll have some special cherry buns when you come home."

So Rupert collects his football and runs off to meet his chums for a kick-about.

RUPERT KICKS THE BALL TOO FAR

As Rupert dribbles with great skill,
His two pals chase him down the hill.

Then Rupert kicks – he's much too keen!
The ball flies into the ravine.

The chums peer in. The ball's in view.
But something glistens down there, too.

As Rupert climbs he takes great care.
The friends watch out for Rupert Bear.

The burglar is forgotten for the moment as Rupert, Bill and Algy play an energetic game of football on the Common. The chums lose track of time, and space, and soon they are chasing the ball over the brow of the hill, towards the ravine. "Do be careful," Bill calls after his pals, but his warning goes unheeded. Rupert tackles the football from Algy and gives it a hefty kick. The ball flies into the air … and tumbles down into the ravine!

The friends kneel on the edge of the ravine and peer in. Their ball is in clear view … but something else catches their eyes, something metallic that glints in the sunlight.

"What do you think it is?" asks Bill.

"Treasure, maybe?" wonders Algy.

"I'll go down and take a closer look," says Rupert, bravely. "Will you watch me?" And before his friends can argue, the little bear has slid down into the ravine.

RUPERT DISCOVERS A ROBOT

Then, in among the rocks and trees,
A robot is what Rupert sees!

There, on his chest, he bears a brand
To show that he was built by hand.

The robot's made by Rupert's chum,
The Old Professor. Will he come?

Off Bill and Algy go at speed
To fetch the help their friend will need.

Bill, Algy and Podgy direct Rupert further down into the gorge. Presently he lands on a ledge by the metal object that has caught their attention. Rupert cranes his neck to look closer, and realises that what he has seen is a robot!

"Goodness gracious!" gasps Rupert. "He must have taken a terrible fall." The poor robot is battered, scratched and dented all over, but Rupert can just make out a brand on his chest.

'*Made by Hand under Patent Number GB0150778, Nutwood,*' Rupert reads out loud. Who in Nutwood would build a robot by hand? "This must be the Old Professor's handiwork!" he realises.

Carefully, Rupert scrambles back out of the ravine and gathers his friends together. "Please hurry and fetch the Old Professor," he tells Bill and Algy. "He will know what to do," he says. "I'll stay here, with the robot."

RUPERT AND BODKIN RESCUE ROBO

The chums return, with Bodkin too,
And Rupert tells him what to do.

The servant pulls the robot loose
But cannot wake him – there's no use.

The Old Professor is prepared!
Poor Robo needs to be repaired.

The robot's circuitry has blown
While he's been walking on his own.

The friends have been gone for some time, and Rupert is beginning to worry when, "Hi!" calls out Bill. "I've brought help." Bill has the Old Professor's servant, Bodkin, with him. With help from Rupert's chums, Bodkin climbs down into the ravine. He tugs at the robot, and manages to free him from the rocky gorge, but the robot shows no sign of waking.

"The Old Professor is waiting for us," says Bodkin. "Robo needs to be repaired at once."

"I'm sorry our football game has been cut short," says Rupert to his pals, but they agree to finish it at school the next day.

Bodkin carries Robo all the way back to the Old Professor's workshop. The Professor takes a close look at Robo. "He's taken quite a tumble," he says. "His circuits have been damaged. He was running an errand and never returned. He must have slipped into the ravine!"

RUPERT SEES ROBO REPAIRED

With welding (and a dab of glue)
The robot's wires are good as new!

And with a gentle shine and buff
The Old Professor's done enough!

The robot's thrilled to meet the friend
Who saved him from a rusty end!

Then Rupert asks him home to tea.
"Yes please!" says Robo, happily.

The Professor sets about repairing Robo's circuitry, which is inside a panel on the robot's back. Several of the wires have come loose and split in places, but the Old Professor is able to weld most of them back together again. Rupert helps the Professor to roll the robot onto his back, and surely enough, with a fizz and a buzz, the robot sparks into life.

The Professor gives Robo a fond brush-over with a soft cloth, and the little robot's eyes slowly open.

"Robo, welcome back!" the Professor beams. "Meet Rupert Bear. He found you in the gully and sent for help. Who knows how long you may have been out there if it hadn't been for him!"

The grateful robot shakes Rupert's hand and thanks him for his kind deed.

"You're welcome," says Rupert. "Would you like to come to tea? Mummy's made some cherry buns!"

The robot is thrilled, and accepts the invitation.

RUPERT AND ROBO FLY HOME

Young Rupert can't believe his eyes!
His friend zooms up into the skies.

Then Robo scoops him from the ground
And soon the pals are homeward bound.

High over chimney pots they go,
But cannot see the thief below …

They come to land, and Mr Bear
Cries, "Rupert, how did you get there?"

Rupert is about to begin the walk home with Robo, when the little robot surprises him by spouting a propellor from the panel on his back, and hovering several feet above the ground!

"You can fly?" Rupert exclaims.

"Yes I can! Would you like to fly with me?" Robo asks his new friend, and before Rupert can reply, Robo has scooped the little bear from the ground and swept him high into the air.

The two pals sail over Nutwood, waving to Rupert's pals who glance up in alarm at seeing the airborne pair.

But what Rupert and Robo don't see is a shady figure slipping out of a nearby window, with a pocketful of stolen jewellery!

"Hi, Daddy!" Rupert cries out, as Robo brings the two of them to a bumpy landing in the lane.

"Good grief, Rupert, what on earth are you doing up there?"

Rupert and Robo

ROBO HELPS AROUND THE HOUSE

Now Robo's keen to lend a hand,
He helps the Bears to work their land!

"My gosh!" cries Dad. "Your shrinking ray
Has zapped that pile of leaves away!"

Inside the cottage, Robo cleans,
And clears his path by any means!

The Bears watch him in great delight,
As Robo puts on extra height!

"This is my new chum, Robo," says Rupert, letting the little robot through the garden gate.

"Rupert helped me out of the ravine," Robo explains. "In return, I'd like to help around the house."

"There's no need; you're a guest," says Mr Bear, but Robo is already clearing up leaves. To the Bears' great surprise, a laser beam shoots from a panel on his chest, and shrinks the leaves into nothing! Then he uses the same beam to grow Dad's wilting plants.

Inside the cottage, Robo wastes no time in putting himself to use. He runs the vacuum cleaner around, lifting chairs and cabinets with ease as he goes. Then he uses his beam to zap away the dust from the vacuum bag!

Suddenly, with a ZOOOOP, Robo's legs shoot upwards so the little robot can reach the tops of the cabinets, too! The Bears are astonished. Robo is doing a spectacular job around the house.

ROBO'S BEAM GOES WRONG!

"Oh no!" the robot gives a cry –
His special beam has gone awry!

It's shrinking things that should be tall,
And growing things that should be small!

As Mr Bear inspects his chair,
He sighs. "I'll never fit on there!"

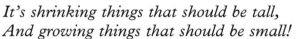

"My coming here was a mistake!
I'm leaving chaos in my wake."

But is it too good to last?

With a fizz and a PSSST, Robo's beam starts to shoot out at all angles, hitting everything in its path.

"Oh, no!" cries Robo, as the beam hits the plate of cherry buns Mrs Bear is carrying, and grows each to the size of a large Victoria sandwich! Robo spins to avoid doing more damage, and his beam hits Mr Bear's armchair, which shrinks to the size of a football. "I'll never fit on there," says Mr Bear with a sigh.

Eventually Robo's beam zaps and fizzles as its power begins to run down. But he feels terribly guilty.

"I'm sorry! I should never have come. I've made such a mess of everything," he frets.

Rupert is quick to console the robot. "Not at all! You've been very helpful."

But Robo cannot be comforted. He decides he must leave and ask the Old Professor to check his wiring once more.

ROBO FOILS THE BURGLAR

Then, startled, Rupert calls out, "Look!"
As from their window leaps the crook!

As Rupert cries out, "Stop, thief! Wait!"
The robber vaults the garden gate.

Then, in a flash, the robot flies
And zaps the robber down to size!

"My beam still works!" the robot cheers.
The burglar almost disappears!

Before Rupert can stop him, Robo bolts from the sitting room and makes for the front door. But the little bear is distracted by a clattering sound coming from the morning room. Rupert runs next-door just in time to see a figure clambering out of the open window, clutching a bulging sack of goods.

"Stop, thief!" he calls out, catching the burglar's attention, and startling Robo. The burglar leaps to the ground outside, and jumps over the garden gate.

"We should call for PC Growler," says Rupert, but Robo takes matters into his own hands! He activates his propellor and zips a few feet into the air.

Taking aim at the burglar, Robo turns on his beam. It shoots in several directions before Robo angles it at the thief. With a loud ZZZAP! the beam hits the thief. He shudders, shakes and shrinks to the size of a small rat!

"Hurrah!" cheers Robo. "My beam still works!"

ROBO TURNS IN THE BURGLAR

The tiny robber tries to flee.
Laughs Robo, "You're no match for me!"

And PC Growler is impressed.
The friends have made a small arrest!

Then Robo says his fond goodbyes
And, with a wave, back home he flies.

Laughs Mummy, "After all that fun,
Would anybody like a bun?"

Robo picks up the burglar between his fingers. The tiny robber wriggles and jiggles and tries to escape, but he stands no chance at his diminutive size. "You're no match for us," the robot chuckles.

Mr Bear has heard all the commotion outside, and has called PC Growler. The policeman is stunned that the pals have managed to capture the burglar.

"This fellow has given me the slip all week," PC Growler says, holding the tiny burglar in his hand.

Robo decides he must say his goodbyes and return to the Old Professor's workshop for more repairs on his beam. He promises to return and put right all the things that he has made the wrong size!

Mummy calls Rupert inside. The little bear is sorry that Robo has left without his tea. But he is soon cheered by the sight of the cake-stand that Mummy and Daddy are carrying into the sitting room. "Would you like a giant cherry bun, Rupert?" laughs Mummy.

RUPERT'S MEMORY TEST

1 What is Mr Bear doing?

2 Which cake ingredient is on the counter-top next to Mrs Bear?

3 Who else is playing football with Rupert and Bill?

4 What has Rupert seen in the ravine here?

5 Who has come to help Rupert?

6 Which of Rupert's friends repairs Robo?

7 What is Rupert wearing in this scene?

8 Who is making a naughty escape?

9 What is Robo shrinking here?

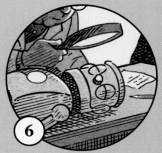

10 Who is in the armchair?

11 What has Robo done to the burglar?

12 What is Mummy holding?

Try this memory test only when you have read the whole story. Each of the pictures above is taken from the story *Rupert and Robo*. Study them carefully, then see if you can answer the questions.

Answers on page 68.

ANSWERS TO PUZZLES

p16, RUPERT LOOKS IN THE ATTIC

There are enough things in the attic to play at least 16 sports and games – table-tennis, lawn tennis, golf, darts, hockey, boxing, roller-skating, croquet, chess, badminton, soccer, rugby, cricket, skipping, sledging and billiards.

p39, RUPERT'S LOST PROPERTY

The answer is FLAG. Rupert loses the flag Mrs Bear has given him.

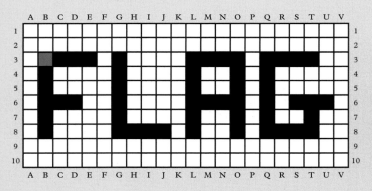

p41, RUPERT AND THE WONDER MACHINE

You have drawn the Old Professor's invention workshop! (See page 60.)

p42, REDIRECTED POST

DINKBO – BODKIN

PIGG-PONN – PONG-PING

LOOTNITE – OTTOLINE

TERPUR – RUPERT

ODGYP – PODGY

p67, RUPERT'S MEMORY TEST

1. Mr Bear is digging.

2. There is an egg on the counter-top.

3. Algy Pug is also playing football.

4. Rupert has seen Robo the robot.

5. Bodkin has come to help Rupert.

6. The Old Professor repairs Robo.

7. Rupert is wearing goggles.

8. The burglar is making a naughty escape!

9. Robo is shrinking a pile of leaves.

10. Mr Bear is in the armchair.

11. Robo has shrunk the burglar!

12. Mummy is holding a cake-stand of giant cherry buns!